For Guthrie, Doris, Elizabeth and Tony
17 Christmases together.
With love, Pa x

T. M.

For cheeky young Theo and Tegan.
Merry Christmas!

L. M.

First edition for the United States and Canada published
in 2007 by Barron's Educational Series, Inc.

A HACHETTE CHILDREN'S BOOK

Text © Tony Mitton 2007
Illustrations © Layn Marlow 2007

ISBN 13: 978-0-7641-6086-8
ISBN 10: 0-7641-6086-9

Library of Congress Control No.: 2007923766

All inquiries should be addressed to:
Barron's Educational Series, Inc.
250 Wireless Boulevard
Hauppauge, New York 11788
www.barronseduc.com

Printed in Singapore
9 8 7 6 5 4 3 2 1

Tony Mitton   Layn Marlow

Christmas Wishes

BARRON'S

On the night before Christmas,
the tree was all hung
With lights and with baubles
that shone as they swung.

The branches were dangled
with glittering things,
While the fairy perched high
with her wand and her wings.

There were shiny, wrapped presents
    beneath the bright tree.
There were green leaves and berries
    and cards hung to see.

For at last it was Christmas!
    And late Christmas Eve
Is when Santa Claus visits,
    or so folks believe.

So we set out a drink
and a Christmassy snack,
With a note saying, "Santa,
please put down your sack . . .

And nibble some Christmas cake,
    give it a try!
For it must be so cold
    in the midwinter sky.

And here are some carrots,
    so crunchy and sweet.
Your hardworking reindeer
    could do with a treat."

Then Dad told a story
and Mom sang a song,
And soon it was time
to be getting along.

So we hung up our stockings
and went to our beds,

As thoughts of our gifts
swam around in our heads.

We lay in our beds
    as the minutes went by,
But all we could do
    was to wriggle and sigh.

To stay up at Christmas
    just wouldn't be right.
But in through our window,
    the moon shone so bright.

It must have been later
than midnight, I guess,
And our heads were all hot
and our beds were a mess,

When outside the window
we heard a faint jingle,
Which made our hearts leap
and our skin start to tingle.

We crept to the window
and, heading our way,
We spied in the sky...

. . . an incredible sleigh!

It was pulled by eight reindeer.
The first had a nose
That glowed quite as brightly
as any red rose!

The sleigh had a cargo
of sacks piled up high,
Which the reindeer had hauled
through the icy, night sky.

And there, as we watched it,
the driver leaned out,
As both of us struggled
to hold back a shout.

His suit was bright red
and his beard was white.
"It's Santa!" we whispered,
with gasps of delight.

Our hearts started thumping.
We didn't think twice.
And downstairs we scuttled—
what mischievous mice!

Old Santa had come down
   the chimney, and now
He was wiping the soot
   from his beard and his brow.

He read all our messages,
   mumbled, "Let's see . . ."
Then he filled up our stockings
   and chuckled with glee.

He nibbled some cake,
    and then, what do you think?
He turned back to face us
    and gave us a wink!

He waggled a finger,
    but smiled as he said,
"What naughty young children!
    Be off now! To bed!"

There was nothing to answer.
   No, nothing to say.
We knew he was right,
   so we had to obey.

We scuttled back up
   to our window, amazed,
To catch a last glimpse,
   and we gazed and we gazed.

Old Santa was giving
   his reindeer a munch
Of the carrots we'd left,
   and some apples to crunch.

Then he reached for the reins
as he jumped in the sleigh,
And he called with a chuckle,
"Now, up and away!"

The reindeer clawed hard
   at the air with their hoofs,
Till the sleigh slowly rose
   to the height of the roofs.

And Santa waved down
   with a cry of delight . . .

"Merry Christmas, my dears . . .

. . . and a very good night!"